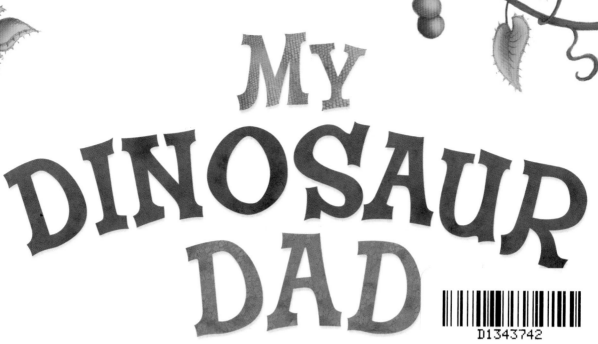

MY DINOSAUR DAD

D1343742

Ruth Paul

■SCHOLASTIC

This dad is **TALL**,

this dad is **SQUAT**.

This dad is
HUGE,

this dad is **NOT**.

This dad is SPIKY,

this dad is **PRICKLY**.

This dad is **KNOBBLY.**

this dad is **TICKLY.**

This dad is **WHISTLING**,

this dad is ROARING.

This dad is whistling and roaring ...

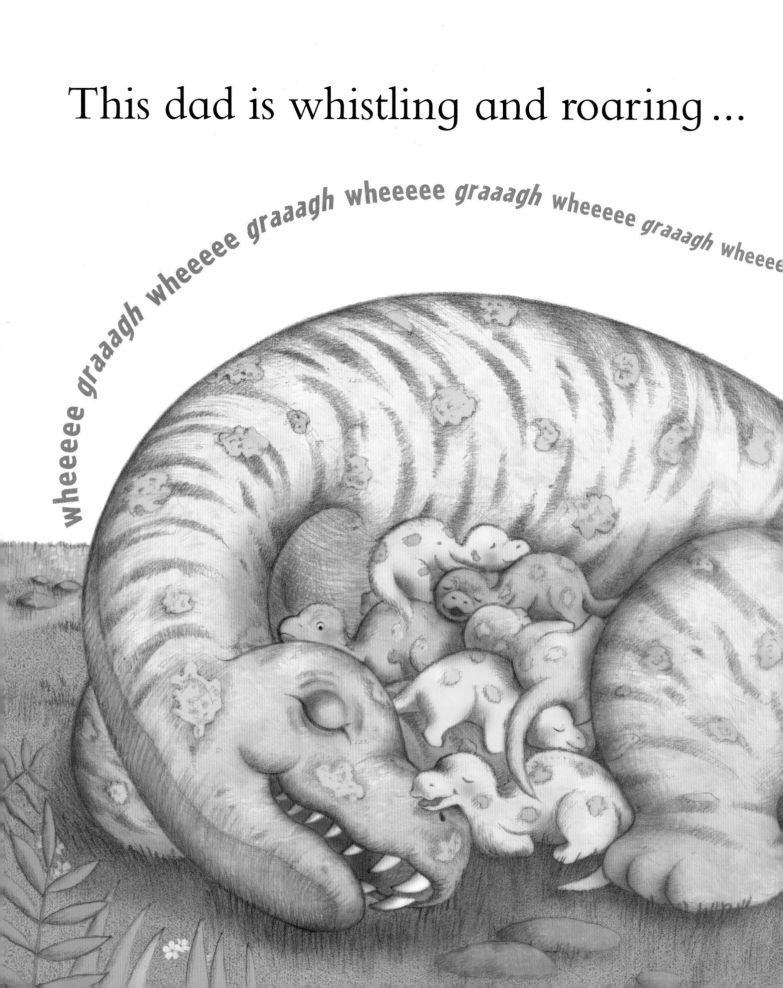

wheeeee graaagh wheeeee graaagh wheeeee graaagh wheeeee graaagh wheeee

and SNORING.

wheeeee *graaagh* wheeeee *graaagh* wheeeee *graaagh* wheeeee *graaagh* wheeeee *graaagh* wheeeee *graaagh* wheeeee *graaagh*

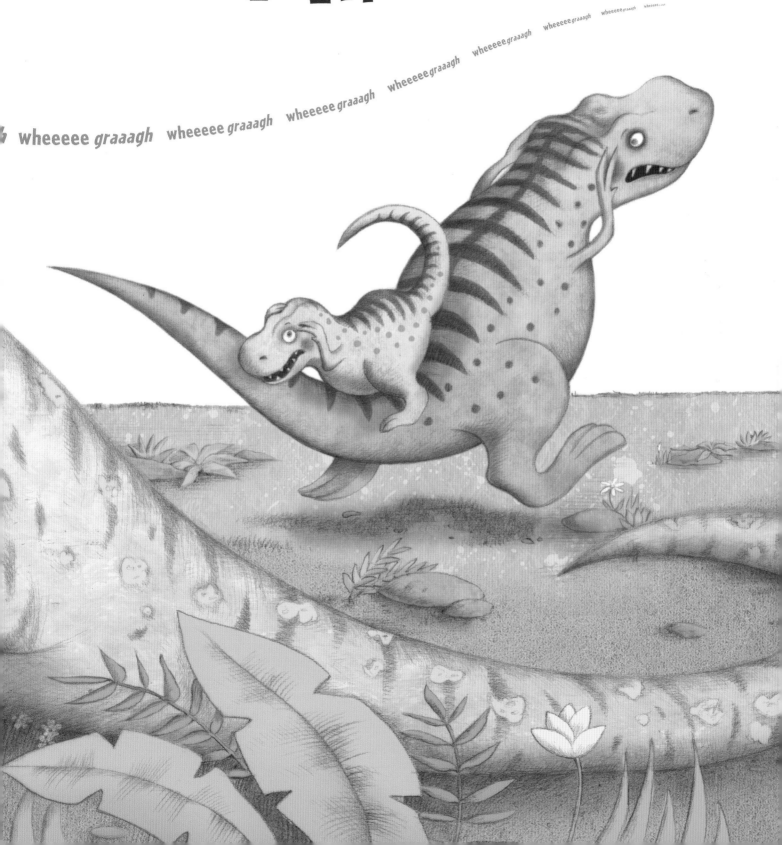

This dad is **CHUNKY**,

this dad is **THINNER**.

This dad is **HUNGRY**

and looking for **dinner**!

This dad is **RACING**,

this dad is **GLIDING**.

This dad is **SWIMMING,**

this dad is
SLIDING.

This dad is
GENTLE,

this dad is
KIND.

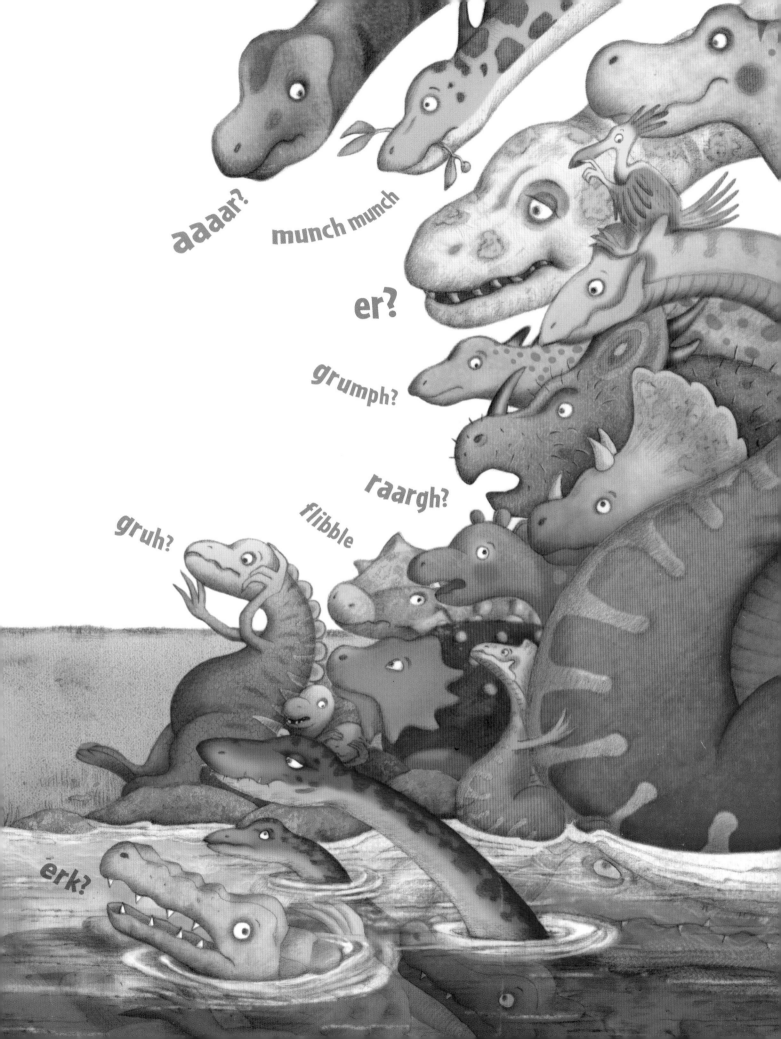

This dad's the **BEST**...

this dad is **mine**.